BEHIND THE FENCE

Congratulations!
Moriah Rhymes

by **Carol K. Taylor**

Carol K Taylor

illustrated by **Irene Joslin**

AuthorHouse™
1663 Liberty Drive, Suite 200
Bloomington, IN 47403
www.authorhouse.com
Phone: 1-800-839-8640

First published by AuthorHouse 1/22/2009

ISBN: 978-1-4389-4352-7 (sc)

Printed in the United States of America
Bloomington, Indiana

This book is printed on acid-free paper.

authorHOUSE®

For Desmond and Jessica

My name is Anna. Behind the fence is where I like to play. My mom said that I will be safe as long as I stay behind the fence.

I could swing higher if I chose to. Maybe I will play in my sandbox.

I can spell my name in the sand and build the tallest sand castle. I will just draw my smile today.

There is my neighbor Mr. Swift with his new puppy.
He said that his name is Beetle.
He also said that I could pet him.
Maybe I will walk closer to the fence.

Mr. Swift said that I could hold him too. Maybe I will walk closer to the fence.

Maybe my mom will let me play with him.
Mr. Swift said that my mom would not mind.
Maybe I will walk closer to the fence.

I always wished for a puppy.
My mom said that I should wait until I turn seven.
Maybe I will walk closer.

"No!" exclaimed Anna.
"My mom said I have to stay behind the fence."

"Mom, Mr. Swift said I could play in his backyard with his puppy," said Anna.
"What did you say and do Anna?" her mother asked.
"I said no and I stayed behind the fence," Anna replied.

"You made the right decision and I am proud of you. I think you are ready for a puppy of your own," said her mother.

Printed in the United States
147108LV00004B